This Cat Came to Stay!

This Cat
Came

FRANKLIN WATTS, Inc.

 699 Madison Ave., New York 21

By ELIZABETH KINSEY

to Stay!

Pictures by DON SIBLEY

To Janet
with love

Contents

1   The Day the Hurdy-Gurdy Came   11

2   Mrs. McGinis   35

3   Mrs. McGinis' Surprise   49

4   A House for Mrs. McGinis   59

5   The Hurdy-Gurdy Man Again   79

6   Mrs. McGinis Moves In   91

7   It Isn't Easy to Find Homes
for Kittens   101

8   Aunt Geneva Changes Her Mind   113

9   The Hurdy-Gurdy Man Comes
Back   130

10   The Hurdy-Gurdy Man Comes
to Stay   153

This Cat Came to Stay!

CHAPTER 1

The Day the
Hurdy-Gurdy Came

It was a quiet time of day in Elm Street. It was just after lunch. All the babies were taking naps. The children were playing quietly.

Patsy Tucker was playing with her friend William Jones under the big tree in William's yard.

Patsy lived next door to William in a small white house with green shutters and a very small yard. She usually lived in the city but now she was staying with her Great-Aunt Geneva while her mother and father were away on a trip. Patsy liked Aunt Geneva and liked to stay with her. She helped with the housework and cooking, and she played with William next door. They usually went to William's house because it was bigger. It had a big porch around it and a big yard with trees and a sand pile and bushes. At the far end there was a tool shed with morning-glory vines growing all over it. It stood in tall grass that William's father never got around to cutting.

Patsy and William were sitting in the shade of the big tree, making a log cabin out of twigs. It had been Patsy's idea to make it. She often had good ideas.

"Who's going to live in this house?" William asked.

"Maybe a bird," said Patsy. "We'll get your father to climb up and put it in the tree and a bird will move in and lay eggs and hatch babies." Patsy liked to make houses.

William looked up into the tree where some birds were hopping about in the branches.

"Those birds all have nests already," he said.

"When they see our house they'll like it better," said Patsy. "It has a roof to keep the rain off."

The birds chirped sleepily. A bee buzzed around and then flew off to a flower bed where William's mother was working. She was on her hands and knees with a big hat on her head and a pair of gloves on her hands, pulling out weeds. She was trying to get a lot done while George, William's little brother, was asleep.

It was very quiet. It was so quiet that it seemed as if everything was going to stay the same all the rest of the afternoon.

"I wonder if anything is going to happen today," said Patsy.

And just then something did. Suddenly, through the quietness, there was a sound of music. It was gay and tinkling.

"What is it?" William asked.

"It sounds like a hurdy-gurdy," said Patsy.

"What's that?" William asked.

"It's a kind of music box," said Patsy. "I've seen them in the city. Come on, let's look for it."

"It sounds as if it's in the next street, behind the house," said William.

But they couldn't go straight through the yards

to find it. They had to go around by the street. So they jumped up and ran to the front.

Aunt Geneva was sitting on her front porch, crocheting. She was always crocheting or knitting when she had nothing else to do. She made mats and pot holders and dishcloths. Her whole house was full of them.

"Where are you going, Patricia?" Aunt Geneva asked. (Patricia was Patsy's real name.)

"We're going to see the hurdy-gurdy," Patsy said.

"Well, stay in the shade," said Aunt Geneva. "It's too hot to be in the sun this time of day." She went on crocheting. Her needle flashed in and out of the mat she was making.

It *was* hot. The heat of the sidewalk burned through the soles of Patsy's and William's sandals. They went around the corner and into the next block. Then they saw the hurdy-gurdy. It was like a little piano on wheels. A man stood beside it and turned a crank. That was what made the music.

When the man got through playing a tune he went to a house and held out his hat, and a lady came out and gave him some money.

"That's a fine way to earn money," said Patsy. "You just play music and people pay you. You can have fun and get money at the same time."

The man smiled at them. He looked nice. His skin was dark and his teeth flashed white when he smiled. He had black curly hair and a shabby coat, and there was a yellow flower stuck in his coat. A piece of honeysuckle vine hung down from his music box. Evidently he liked flowers.

He started to play another tune. As he played he looked around as though he were trying to find something.

"Isn't he supposed to have a monkey?" William asked.

"Sometimes they have monkeys," said Patsy. "Maybe that's what he's looking for." But there was no monkey in sight.

"Tinkle, tinkle, tinkle," went the music. Some more children came out to listen. Some of them began to sing and dance. Others ran to their mothers to get money to give the man.

"Come to our street," Patsy said. "I'll get

money from Aunt Geneva." She beckoned to show him which way to come.

The man followed Patsy and William, pulling his music box on its wheels. He kept looking into all the yards they passed. Every now and then he stopped and played another tune. At last they came around the corner into Elm Street, and the man began to play again.

"Tinkle, tinkle," went the music. But suddenly a lady with a very cross face came out of a house.

"Go away," she said. "You'll wake up the baby. This is no time of day to play music!"

The man looked worried. He said something to the lady. But it didn't sound like English and the lady didn't understand him. She shook her head and waved her hand to show that he was to go away. Then some more ladies came out and looked cross. There were lots of babies on Elm Street and they were all supposed to be asleep.

The man looked frightened. He grabbed the handles of the hurdy-gurdy and went away as fast as he could.

Patsy felt sorry for him. She waved to him until he was out of sight. Then she and William went back to finish their log cabin.

"He looked like a nice man," said William.

"Yes," said Patsy. "I wish he would stay here so we could hear that music box all the time. It's a shame to chase him away just because some babies are sleeping."

"Well, sometimes it's pretty hard to get them to sleep," said William. He knew, because he had a little brother.

And just then they heard George's voice. He had waked up. Mrs. Jones got up from the flower bed and took off her gloves and went into the house. Pretty soon she came back with George.

"Would you mind him for a while, William?" she said. "I want to work in the garden a little longer and that hurdy-gurdy woke him up." She put George down beside them and started to pull up some more weeds.

"See what I mean?" said William.

Patsy saw what he meant. George was a very nice little boy, and he loved Patsy and William. He always wanted to follow them around and

do everything they did. Now he toddled over to help make the log cabin.

"Make house," he said, and he gave it a swat and knocked it flat.

He smiled. "House all gone," he said, and sat down to play with the sticks.

"What shall we do now?" William asked.

"We could play hide and seek while he's doing that," said Patsy.

But as soon as they started to play, he came too. When it was Patsy's turn to hide, he showed William where she was.

"Patsy in dere," he said.

"We can't play anything with him around," said William.

"Let's put him in the sandbox," said Patsy.

"We can't leave him alone in there," said William. "The last time I did it he ate some sand."

Somebody would have to watch George. But who?

"I'll think of something," said Patsy. She usually did. She stood still and thought, and pretty soon she had an idea.

"Let's make the sandbox home base," she said. "While you're hiding I can stay here and watch George, and while I'm hiding you can watch him."

"That's a good idea," said William. So Patsy sat down to play with George, and William crept off among the bushes.

Patsy counted to a hundred. Then she called, "Here I come, ready or not!"

Then she gave George the pail and shovel and said, "Now you dig a pail full of sand before I come back."

"Me dig sand," said George, and he got very busy.

Patsy walked slowly around the garden, looking carefully under the bushes for William. At last, off in a corner by the tool shed where the grass grew tall, she saw something moving.

"Probably William is hidden in there," she thought. She walked very quietly toward the tool shed.

"I spy William!" she shouted.

Suddenly William dashed out from behind a

tree and ran for the sandbox. He hadn't been in the grass at all.

But what *was* in the grass?

"Meow!" said a voice, and out walked a cat, waving her tail in the air. She was a handsome cat, gray all over, with yellow eyes.

"Hello, cat," said Patsy. "Where did you come from?"

The cat did not answer. She came to Patsy and rubbed against her leg.

"Home free!" shouted William, who had reached the sandbox by this time. "What are you doing over there?"

"There's a cat," said Patsy.

William came to look at it. "Meow," said the cat, rubbing herself against William's legs.

"Whose cat is she?" William asked. "I never saw her before."

"I don't know," said Patsy. "Whose cat are you, cat?"

The cat just kept on saying "Meow."

"She's a nice cat," said Patsy.

"Well, she'd better go home before George sees her," said William. "Go home, cat."

The cat just stood there.

"Let's go inside the house where she can't see us," said William.

They ran to the house and hurried to shut the screen door so the cat couldn't get in. The cat dashed after them and ran up the back steps. She stood at the door crying "Meow" very loudly.

"I wonder what she's saying," said William.

"I bet I know," said Patsy. "Probably she's saying, 'The people I belong to have gone away and I haven't had my lunch. I would like some milk.'"

27

"How do you know?" William asked.

"Well, if I were a cat and said 'Meow' like that, that is what it would mean," said Patsy.

So William got a bottle of milk out of the refrigerator and poured some into a saucer and put it on the floor. Then he and Patsy let the cat into the kitchen. She ran to the saucer and drank all the milk as fast as she could.

"Meow!" she said.

"That means thanks," said Patsy.

"I'm glad I'm not a cat," said William. "I'd hate to have to use the same word for everything."

"She can probably purr too," said Patsy. And she sat down on the floor and took the cat in her lap. The cat purred.

Just then William's mother came in from the garden and saw the cat. She got very excited.

"Where did that cat come from?" she demanded. "Put it out at once. If you feed it, it will never go away. Oh, dear, you *have* fed it! You naughty children! Shoo, cat!"

She opened the door to let the cat out, but before the cat could go outside again, Mrs. Jones spied George in the sandbox. He was pouring sand over his hair.

"Oh, *now* look what the baby is doing!" she exclaimed. And she ran out and grabbed him and brought him in.

As soon as George saw the cat he began to shout happily, "Pussy! Pussy!" He grabbed the cat's tail and gave it a good hard pull.

"EE-OW!" said the cat, leaping away.

"That's three words she knows," said Patsy.

"You must take that cat away!" said Mrs. Jones. "It's just a stray cat and doesn't belong to anybody around here."

"Then can't we keep it, Mama?" William asked.

"No, William," said his mother. "It seems like a nice cat, but George would keep pulling its tail and it would scratch him. You will have to get it out of here."

"I'll go and see if I can keep it," said Patsy.

She picked up the cat and went out across the garden and through a hole in the fence. Her Aunt Geneva was in the kitchen mixing a cake. She made very good cakes.

"You're just in time to help me scrape the bowl," she said. And then she saw the cat.

"What's that you have there?" she asked.

"It's a stray cat," said Patsy.

"A stray cat!" said Aunt Geneva. "Well, take it out of the house at once. It must belong to somebody. Just let it go and it will find its way home."

"No," said Patsy. "She doesn't belong to anybody around here. Couldn't we keep her?"

"No, indeed," said Aunt Geneva, beating

the batter steadily with her wooden spoon.

Patsy was surprised. Usually Aunt Geneva let her do almost anything she wanted.

"But why not?" she asked.

"Because it isn't ours," said Aunt Geneva.

"But if she has no home and we keep her, then she will be ours," said Patsy.

"No, it won't," said Aunt Geneva.

Patsy was very fond of Aunt Geneva, but this time she just didn't understand her.

"But why not?" she asked again.

"Because we don't want any cats here," said Aunt Geneva.

Patsy thought differently, but there didn't seem to be much she could do about it. She picked up the cat and went outside. What could she do? She couldn't keep the cat if Aunt Geneva said no. But where would the cat go? They couldn't just turn her out.

31

"I'll think of something," she said to herself.

As she stood there thinking, she heard a terrible racket next door. George was howling, and his mother was telling him to stop.

"Please stop crying, George," she said. "Mother must comb your hair and get all the nasty sand out of it."

Patsy looked through the hole in the fence. Mrs. Jones was trying to comb the baby's hair. He was yelling and trying to get away.

"Maybe if I let him look at the cat he'll stop yelling," Patsy thought, and she went over to the Joneses' back porch.

As soon as George saw the cat he stopped crying and smiled.

"Pussy come back!" he said.

And he quieted down and let his mother comb his hair. Patsy sat beside him and George stroked the cat's soft fur.

"Well, I'm glad you brought her back," said
Mrs. Jones. "I just couldn't do a thing with
George. And she does seem like a nice cat."

"Can we keep her, then?" William asked.

"Well, all right," his mother said, "until you

find out where she belongs. But you will have to feed her and take care of her. I have too much to do already."

"I will, Mama," said William.

"And I'll help you," said Patsy. "Let's feed her now."

"There's a dish of meat scraps in the refrigerator," said Mrs. Jones. "You may take that."

They brought the dish, and the cat gobbled up the food. She was quite hungry. Then she sat down to wash herself.

By now Mrs. Jones had finished combing George's hair.

"Nice pussy!" George said, and he reached out and grabbed the cat's tail.

"Ee-ow!" she squawked, jumping away.

"That's the only trouble," said Mrs. Jones. "I do hope he will learn not to do that. One of these days she may scratch him."

34

CHAPTER 2

Mrs. McGinis

Patsy and William asked all the people they knew whether they had lost a gray cat with yellow eyes, but nobody had. Suddenly the cat had appeared from the back of the garden. Nobody knew where she had come from and nobody wanted her.

Patsy asked Aunt Geneva a few more times whether they couldn't have her.

"No, indeed," said Aunt Geneva.

"But why not?" Patsy asked.

"We don't need a cat," said Aunt Geneva.

"But couldn't we have her anyway, just because we like her?" said Patsy.

"No," said Aunt Geneva.

"Why not?" Patsy asked.

"Well, to tell you the truth, Patricia," said Aunt Geneva, "I don't like cats."

Patsy was amazed. Not like cats! How could anybody not like cats? But then she remembered that grownups were sometimes funny that way. Her mother didn't like chocolate. And once they had had a visitor who didn't like ice cream! There wasn't much sense to that.

"Why not, Aunt Geneva?" she asked.

"Oh, they jump on tables, and they scratch the furniture and tangle the yarn when you're crocheting. Once we had a cat that clawed down all the mats." And she looked around the room at all the little crocheted mats on the tables. "What a mess a cat would make here!" she said.

Patsy thought a cat was more important than table mats, but she loved Aunt Geneva so she didn't ask about keeping the cat again. Anyway, the cat was very happy at William's house. Every day Patsy went to help him take care of her.

They made her a bed in an old peach basket on the back porch and fed her canned sardines and milk and any scraps that William's mother had. Pretty soon the cat began to get fat. She was very good. She didn't scratch the furniture or jump on tables. Her gray coat was shiny and clean. She was always washing herself. They decided to call her Mrs. McGinis. Patsy thought that was a nice, dignified name.

After a few weeks it seemed as if Mrs. McGinis had always lived in the Joneses' house. The only trouble was that George could not, or would not, learn to leave her tail alone. Patsy and William told him and told him that he mustn't pull Mrs.

McGinis' tail. But George loved Mrs. McGinis very much and was always running after her.

"Tum here, nice pussy," he would say sweetly, and then he would reach for that fascinating tail.

One day, as Patsy was helping Aunt Geneva make cookies, she heard a fearful noise from the house next door. George was yelling.

"I think I'll go and see what's the matter with George," said Patsy. "Seems as if his mother can't do a thing with him."

She went through the hole in the fence, and there on the back porch was George, howling. His mother was calling, "Here, kitty, kitty!" At the same time she was trying to put mercurochrome on his arm. And William was inside the house, running up and down stairs and moving chairs about and making a terrific noise.

"What's the matter?" Patsy asked.

"Wow!" howled George. "Pussy go way fah way!"

"Please stop crying, George," his mother said.

George only howled louder.

"I can't understand you when you cry like that," said Patsy.

George stopped crying. There was a red streak on his arm. He looked down at it and sniffed. "Pussy go way fah way," he said.

"Oh," said Patsy. "Your pussy's gone way far away. Did you pull her tail?"

"Yes," said Mrs. Jones, "I am afraid George pulled her tail once too often. She scratched him, and then she ran away. I think it will be a good thing if she stays away. He won't learn not to pull her tail, and I can't have her scratching him."

Patsy said, "Maybe if she scratches him a few times, he'll learn not to pull her tail."

"No, he's too young to learn a thing like that," said Mrs. Jones. "It would only frighten him. The cat has run away, and she can stay away."

At this George began to yell again, so loudly that his mother put her hands over her ears. "All right, George," she shouted over his yelling, "stop crying and we'll all look for the pussy."

Just then William came clattering down the stairs and shouted, "I can't find her!"

Patsy could see what was the matter. They were all making so much noise that the cat was afraid to come back.

"Maybe if we all keep quiet the pussy will come back," she suggested.

"That's a very good idea," said Mrs. Jones, but George was crying so hard he didn't even hear her.

"Keep still!" William shouted, but that only made the baby roar more loudly.

Patsy saw that she must do something herself.

"Let's go very quietly and look for her in the
garden," she said.

Patsy and William went into the garden. They
walked about and searched under the bushes.
They looked in the trees and in the swing and in

the sand pile. They looked in the garage and in the hedge. No Mrs. McGinis.

"I wonder why she should suddenly run away," said Patsy. "She never did it before."

"Maybe she just got tired of having her tail pulled," said William. "I would if I had a tail."

"No, she must have some special reason," said Patsy.

"Maybe she was sorry she scratched him and was afraid Mama would scold her," said William.

"I don't think cats are sorry," said Patsy. "If they do something, it's because they mean to do it."

"Well, what are we going to do about George?" William asked. "We can't let him just go on yelling."

"We'll keep our eyes open and something will turn up," said Patsy.

And just then something did. Off in the tall grass by the tool shed Patsy saw something moving. She hurried over to look.

There among the weeds was a turtle. He had a brown shell. A little leathery face, four legs and a pointed tail stuck out of his shell.

"Hello, turtle," said Patsy.

44

The turtle didn't answer. He took one look at Patsy and started to go away.

"Wait a minute, turtle," said Patsy.

The turtle stopped. He pulled his head and tail and all his legs into the shell and sat very still. He looked like a little brown box sitting in the grass.

Patsy picked him up.

"Let's take him to see George," she said to William. "Maybe this will keep him quiet."

"That's a good idea," said William. "We'll put him in a tub so he can't get away."

"Where can we get a tub?" Patsy asked.

"In the tool shed," said William, and he pushed open the door.

All kinds of things were in the shed. William rummaged around and pretty soon he found an old dishpan with the enamel chipped off the bottom. It was plenty good enough for the turtle. They put some water in the bottom so that the turtle could wade and William put in a rock and some earth so he could climb out of the water if he wanted to. Then they took the turtle and his tub to the back porch, where George was still crying for Mrs. McGinis.

"Look, George," said Patsy, "see what we brought you."

"It's a turtle," said William.

George smiled. "Turkle," he said.

The turtle opened his shell and looked around. Then he put out his legs and tail and began to walk across the tub.

George reached in to grab the turtle's tail. But the turtle quickly pulled into his shell and made himself into a little box again.

"Turkle all gone," said George.

"Just sit very quietly and watch," said Patsy, "and pretty soon the turtle will come out."

They all sat and watched, and sure enough, the turtle did.

Mrs. Jones came out to see what they were all so quiet about, and she was pleased. Then she got some raisins and William put them on the rock and the turtle ate them.

George was pleased. "Turkle eat," he said.

The turtle seemed pleased, too, with the raisins.

And whenever George reached out to grab its tail, it closed itself up again. It was a very good pet for George.

CHAPTER 3

Mrs. McGinis' Surprise

But where was Mrs. McGinis?

All the rest of the afternoon Patsy and William looked for her, but she was nowhere around. They called and called, but no answering voice said "Meow," or "Prrr," or even "Ee-ow!"

At last Aunt Geneva called Patsy to come and help put the cookies in the cooky jar. William went along, too.

After they had tasted a few cookies to make sure they were all right, it was supper time. William's mother called him to come home. William remembered Mrs. McGinis. "I wonder where she is," he said sadly.

"Don't worry about that cat," said Aunt Geneva, who was sitting in the kitchen crocheting a dishcloth while the supper cooked. "Cats can always take care of themselves."

But William was almost ready to cry. "She won't have any supper if she doesn't come in now," he said.

"I know what you can do," said Patsy. "Put some food out tonight before you go to bed. Then she can come and get it in the middle of the night."

"Okay, that's a good idea," said William, and he went home feeling much better.

Very early the next morning Patsy woke up. It was very quiet. Aunt Geneva was still asleep. Downstairs the big clock went bong, bong, bong,

bong, bong, bong. Only six bongs. Patsy knew it was not time to get up yet. She shut her eyes and tried to go to sleep again, but her eyes wouldn't stay shut.

She got out of bed quietly and put on her slippers. They were fur slippers and she could walk in them without making a sound. She tiptoed downstairs to the kitchen. She opened the kitchen door and looked out into the garden. The sun was just coming up. It shone on the drops of dew that hung from the tips of the grass blades. It shone on the bottles of milk that the milkman had left on the back steps.

Patsy wondered whether Mrs. McGinis had come in the night to eat the supper William had put out for her. Very quietly she stepped out into the garden. She climbed through the hole in the fence and went across William's yard. The grass was long and wet. Mr. Jones had not cut it because the lawn mower was broken. On the lowest step of the house was an empty saucer. Mrs. McGinis had had her supper.

Patsy walked back through the quiet garden. A robin was getting its breakfast. It stood in the grass and pulled up a worm. Then it flew to a bush and there was a loud chirping.

"That bird is getting breakfast for its children," said Patsy. "I wish somebody would give me some breakfast. Only not worms."

Then she thought, "Well, my goodness, I guess I have sense enough to get my own breakfast."

Back home, she carried the bottles of milk inside. She poured milk into a glass and got some cookies from the cooky jar and went out on the back steps to eat her breakfast.

All of a sudden something soft brushed the back of her neck. She looked around, and there was Mrs. McGinis. She had come up behind Patsy and tickled the back of Patsy's neck with her tail!

"Hello, Mrs. McGinis," said Patsy.

"Meow," said Mrs. McGinis. She walked back and forth and rubbed herself against Patsy, not making a sound with her feet.

"You have fur slippers too," said Patsy. "That's why I didn't hear you."

"Prrr," said Mrs. McGinis, pushing her head against Patsy's arm.

"Where have you been all this time?" Patsy asked.

"Meow," said Mrs. McGinis.

"That's no way to talk to me," said Patsy. "I asked you a question. William has been very worried about you. I can understand that you don't want your tail pulled, but you should at least let William or me know where you're going."

Mrs. McGinis paid no attention to all this talk. Instead she tried to put her head inside Patsy's glass of milk.

"Oh, you're hungry," said Patsy. "Well, all right. Just *wait* a minute."

Patsy got a saucer and poured some milk into it and put it on the step. Mrs. McGinis ran to it and lapped it all up.

"Meow," she said again, running back and forth and waving her tail in the air.

"What is it now?" Patsy asked.

Mrs. McGinis ran down the steps. Then she turned around and looked back to see if Patsy was coming. Patsy followed her. The cat ran around the house to the side porch. She squeezed underneath it.

Patsy squatted down and looked. Something was wriggling in there. Something very small that said "Meow!" in a tiny squeaky voice.

"Oh!" said Patsy. "Oh! You have *kittens* in there! Oh, Mrs. McGinis, how *nice!* No wonder you ran away. Of course you didn't want your tail pulled and you didn't want a lot of noise! You were smart to hide them in there. Do you mind if I hold one?"

And she reached in to pick up a kitten. There were three of them.

But Mrs. McGinis said, "Mrrow!" in a warning voice. She put her paw on Patsy's hand.

"Okay, I won't if you don't want me to," said Patsy. "And I suppose you'd like to keep your kittens a secret."

"Meow," said Mrs. McGinis.

"All right," said Patsy. "Only of course I'll have to tell William. After all, you *are* a member of his family. And you can't stay here very long."

"Meow?" said Mrs. McGinis.

"I'm afraid not," said Patsy. "Aunt Geneva

doesn't like cats. It's silly, but that's the way it is."

And Patsy walked back to the kitchen, leaving Mrs. McGinis alone with her family.

CHAPTER 4

A House for Mrs. McGinis

Slowly and thoughtfully, Patsy went upstairs. She took off her fur slippers, put on her daytime shoes with leather soles and heels, and went down again. Pretty soon Aunt Geneva came into the kitchen and got breakfast. Of course Patsy had some too, just to keep her company. Before she knew it she had eaten an egg and some cereal and toast and jam and another glass of milk. And all the time she wondered what she ought to do about Mrs. McGinis.

"Maybe Aunt Geneva will change her mind about cats and let them all stay," she thought.

"I wish *we* had a cat," she said out loud, just to see.

"Mercy!" said Aunt Geneva. "Don't even mention it! I just can't stand cats!"

So Patsy knew that was no use.

"I'll think of something," she said to herself.

After breakfast she went to look for William. She found him standing on the sidewalk. Beside him was a beautiful tricycle. It was shiny and red and it looked brand-new.

"Where did you get that?" Patsy asked.

"My father brought it last night," said William. "My mother wanted him to buy a new lawn mower but he got this instead."

"That's nice," said Patsy. "Let's go for a ride."

"I can't," said William.

"Why not, for goodness' sake?" Patsy asked.

60

He pointed to George who was sitting on the front lawn sucking his thumb.

"When I try to ride it," said William, "my brother yells. He wants to ride it too. And he's too small. And Mama says I have to mind him."

"Couldn't he stand on the back and hold on while you ride?" Patsy asked.

"We could try it," said William.

He got on the bike. Patsy stood George on the back and told him to hold on. William pedaled slowly along the sidewalk. But suddenly George forgot to hold on. Bump! Down he went.

"Wow!" he roared, sitting there with the tears rolling down his face.

Patsy picked him up and put him on the grass. "You're too small," she told him. "You sit there and watch and I'll show you how to hold on." She stood on the back and William pedaled off very fast, ringing the bell. It was wonderful.

But George didn't like it. "Wow!" he cried.

Mrs. Jones put her head out. "What are you doing to him?" she called. "I thought I told you to mind him."

"We tried to teach him to ride," said Patsy, "but he fell off. Now he's watching me to see how it's done."

But Mrs. Jones called out, "William, I'm too busy to mind George right now. You'll have to ride your bike while he's taking his nap."

So they got off the bike and took George into the back yard and put him in the sandbox.

"Now there's nothing to do," said William.

"Oh, I wouldn't say that," said Patsy. "There's always something to do. Come over here where the baby can't hear us and I'll tell you a secret." They walked away and Patsy whispered, "I know where Mrs. McGinis is."

"You do!" said William. "Where?"

"Sh! Sh!" said Patsy. "I promised I wouldn't tell anybody but you. She's under my side porch. And she's got three kittens!"

"Yippee!" shouted William.

Patsy shook her head at him. "You'll just *have* to be more quiet," she said. "We can't have the whole neighborhood bothering those kittens. Now we'll have to think up a good place to keep them."

"Why can't we bring them over to my porch?" said William. "I'll make a bed for them in a box, and I'll feed them and take good care of them."

"Really, William," said Patsy, "I'm surprised at you. George would squeeze them and pull their tails, and Mrs. McGinis would scratch him, and goodness knows what would happen."

"That's right," said William. "We'll have to think of a place for them."

And they sat down and began to think. The harder they thought, the fewer ideas they had.

Finally Patsy said, "We might as well be doing something while we're thinking. It's no use just sitting here."

"Okay, let's play ball," said William.

He got his ball and threw it to Patsy, and she hit it back to him with a stick. It went through the door of the tool shed, which William had left open the day before when he got the dishpan.

"Oh, boy, now look what you did," said William. "We'll have a fine time finding that ball."

"What do you mean?" Patsy asked. "It's just in the tool shed."

"I guess you don't know our tool shed," said William. "My father puts everything in there that he doesn't want around the house. And my mother puts everything in that *she* doesn't want. We can't ever find that ball."

"Nonsense," said Patsy. "There's no such word as can't. Come on, let's look." And she walked in.

The tool shed was dark and very full. Patsy thought it was queer to call it a tool shed. There didn't seem to be any tools anywhere. Instead, piled on top of each other were old chairs with broken legs that William said his father was going to fix some time. Patsy could see window

shades that were partly good too, and jam jars and automobile parts, old bathing suits, pieces of rope, and lots of other things.

"I see what you mean about not finding the ball," said Patsy. "We'll have to take some of the stuff outside."

So she and William began pulling things out.

They dragged out some chairs, a lawn mower, a
baby's canvas bathtub without any canvas, a
lampshade with castles painted on it, a heap of
old magazines, and a portable phonograph with
the cover broken off. They piled them up on the
lawn.

They worked and worked, and after a long time

they got the place pretty well cleared out. There was nothing much left in the tool shed but an old sofa with the stuffing sticking out of the arms, a couple of heavy tables which they couldn't move, and a little wagon with three wheels. In the wagon was the ball!

"You see, I told you we'd find it," said Patsy.

William was outside staring at the pile of stuff on the lawn.

"I don't see how we're going to get all this back again," he said gloomily.

Patsy didn't answer. She was inside the tool shed looking around. Now that all the junk was out of it, it was a very nice little house. It was pretty dirty, of course. The window was covered with cobwebs. The floor was littered with dust and papers and old chair legs. But the shed could easily be cleaned up, Patsy decided.

"I have an idea," she called to William. "This would make a fine place for Mrs. McGinis and her kittens!"

William came back and looked around. "You're right," he said, "they could sleep on that sofa. But what about George?"

"He wouldn't be able to open the door," said Patsy. "And Mrs. McGinis could get in and out through the window."

But William shook his head. "My mother wouldn't let me leave all that stuff on the lawn," he said.

Patsy came out and looked at the big pile they had made. There really were a lot of things there. She thought a while and then she said, "Maybe your mother will be glad we took all this out. Sometimes grownups put things away and forget about them. I was helping my mother clean the attic once and she found a lot of stuff she wanted.

Come on." She picked up the lampshade with castles painted on it and started for the house.

On the way they passed George in the sand pile. He was pouring sand down inside the front of his shirt.

"Stop that, George," said William, and he stood him up to shake the sand out. George opened his mouth to howl.

"Wait a minute," said Patsy, "here's something he'll like."

She ran back and got the little red wagon and gave it to George. Because it had only three wheels it wouldn't stand up. So George turned it upside down and began spinning the wheels around.

"Wheels go wound," he said happily.

Mrs. Jones was in the kitchen cutting up beans for lunch.

"What have you children been doing?" she called.

"Cleaning out the tool shed," said William.

"Cleaning the tool shed!" Mrs. Jones cried. "Who told you to do that?"

"We were looking for our ball," said Patsy. "See what we found, Mrs. Jones!"

She held up the lampshade.

"Well, my gracious, where did you get that?"

Mrs. Jones demanded. "I'd forgotten all about it. Why, it's lovely!"

"It was in the tool shed," said William. "We thought you didn't want it."

"Of course I want it," said his mother, taking it from Patsy. "Your father must have put it there. What else is out there?"

"Oh, lots of stuff," said Patsy. "We got it all out."

"Got it all out!" cried Mrs. Jones. "Where is it?"

She put down the beans and ran outside. William and Patsy followed right along.

"My goodness!" Mrs. Jones exclaimed. "What ever got into you children? Why, look at those chairs! I bought them at an auction and your father promised to fix them. And look at that bathtub! Why, all it needs is some new canvas! The idea of throwing it in there!"

And she began to carry the things into the house.

"Then you don't want us to put it all back?" William asked.

"No, indeed, not till I have had a chance to look it over," said his mother. "Look, here's the lawn mower. There's just one blade broken. Your father can easily have that fixed, and we can have the grass cut."

Just then Aunt Geneva came over to see what was going on.

"Patricia, I hope you're not bothering Mrs. Jones," she began. And then she saw the pile of things on the lawn. "Why, where did you get that beautiful coal scuttle?" she asked.

"Oh, that old thing," said Mrs. Jones. "Would you like it? The children started cleaning out the shed and look at what my husband just threw in there!"

"They're beautiful," said Aunt Geneva, and she started helping Mrs. Jones carry the things to the house. Pretty soon they had the pile nearly cleaned up.

"And those old magazines," said Mrs. Jones. "The Boy Scouts were around looking for paper the other day. They can have them."

When William's father got home at lunch-time he was surprised to see a lot of broken chairs on the back porch.

"The children found them in the tool shed," Mrs. Jones said. "I'd like you to fix them."

"What, that junk!" exclaimed Mr. Jones.

"They're not junk, they're valuable antiques," said Mrs. Jones. "And look, here's the lawn mower. You can easily have it fixed."

Mr. Jones looked at the lawn mower as if he had a pain. Then he looked in the trash barrels.

"Who said you could throw out those valuable automobile parts?" he demanded.

"What, that junk?" said his wife. "I don't see what you need it for. You didn't even know it was there."

"And those magazines!" exclaimed Mr. Jones. "Why, they're twenty years old! They're rare books by now!"

He lugged all the things into the garage and sat down and read some of the old magazines.

All this time George had been playing with the little red wagon, and when he had to come to lunch he brought it along. When his father saw the wagon, he took it away from George and said he would put a fourth wheel on it, perhaps that evening.

But George howled so loudly that his father had to give the wagon to him. Then Mr. Jones went right out to the garage and got the fourth

75

wheel, which had been lying around there for a year or so. He put it on the wagon then and there!

Mrs. Jones was very much pleased. "This is the best way I ever saw of getting things fixed," she said to Patsy and William. "You children deserve a reward. This afternoon we'll all have ice cream."

"There's something else we'd rather have," said Patsy.

"Something you'd rather have?" Mrs. Jones asked. "What can it be?"

"May we have the tool shed for ourselves?" asked Patsy.

"Yes," said William, "please let us have the tool shed. Only don't tell anybody. It's a secret."

"Well, I don't see why you shouldn't have the tool shed to play in," said his mother. "Only why should it be a secret?"

"We promised," said Patsy.

"Well, all right, if you don't do any mischief," said Mrs. Jones. "And you'll have to clean it out. It's awfully dirty."

"Oh, we don't mind that," said William.

"Goody," said Patsy, as they ran off to get brooms and rags. "Now we can fix up a nice house."

CHAPTER 5

The Hurdy-Gurdy Man
Again

Patsy and William spent all afternoon cleaning the tool shed. They swept the floor. They wiped dirt off the walls, as high as they could reach. They washed the little window. Patsy got some of the jam jars Mrs. Jones had thrown in the ash can and put flowers in them. She found an old bathmat and put it on the floor for a rug. The house was ready for Mrs. McGinis and the kittens.

Now came the problem of moving them in.

For a couple of hours after lunch, George had slept soundly. But now he was sitting happily in the sand pile, spinning the four wheels of his wagon. Patsy and William could not carry the kittens through the garden without having him see them. And of course as soon as he did he would howl until he was allowed to play with them. They would just have to wait until he went to bed again.

"Something is always interfering with us," said William.

"Always look on the bright side," said Patsy. "Why don't we ride your new bike?"

"All right," said William, "let's go."

They went out to the front sidewalk, but the bike was nowhere in sight.

"I guess somebody borrowed it," said William. "We'll have to look for it."

They walked up the street looking in all

the front yards, but no bright new tricycle was to be seen, nor any children either. Finally they did see a couple of big boys playing ball.

"Where has everybody gone?" William asked them.

"They went that way," said one of the boys, pointing.

Patsy and William went the way the boy had showed them. They walked and walked. After a while they began to hear the gay, tinkling sound of music.

"Oh, it's the hurdy-gurdy again!" said Patsy. "Come on!"

They began to run. Pretty soon they saw the man with his music box. He had a blue flower stuck in his coat and a long string of morning-glories hanging down from the hurdy-gurdy. And following him was a crowd of children, walking and riding on bikes and scooters and wagons.

William looked at all the bikes. Pretty soon he saw a boy riding a shiny new tricycle.

"That's my bike," said William.

"Yes, I know," said the boy. "I borrowed it. I was going to bring it back."

"Well, may I have it now, please?" said William.

"Sure," said the boy, getting off.

William was very happy to find his bike. He got on it and Patsy stood on the back and they followed the man. As soon as he had played a tune he went to all the houses and people gave him money. Nobody chased him,—perhaps because it wasn't naptime, and perhaps because there weren't many babies on this street. But he kept looking anxiously around. He peered into every front yard and on every porch.

"What's he looking for?" William wondered.

"Maybe he's afraid somebody will chase him away," said Patsy.

"But nobody is chasing him," said William.

"Well, I guess he's looking at the flowers in the gardens," said Patsy. "He likes flowers."

"My father doesn't," said William. "He says the only way he can tell the difference between the weeds and the flowers is to pull them all up and the ones that grow again are the weeds."

They followed the hurdy-gurdy man for quite a way. Patsy wished he would come to Elm Street, but he kept going farther and farther away. At last they turned around and started home again. William pedaled very fast, his legs going up and down like a steam engine. Patsy held on tight. They went so fast her hair flew straight out behind her in the wind they made.

"This is a good bike," she shouted in William's ear, and William nodded. He was going too fast to talk.

It wasn't too near George's bedtime, and they thought they would have a chance to ride up and down some more while he played with his wagon in the sand pile.

William's father had been very busy mending the lawn mower. Now he was sitting on the porch reading some of the old magazines the children had found in the tool shed. His wife had said he must get rid of them, and he wanted to look them over first to make sure he didn't throw out something valuable.

"This is a good bike, Dad," William called, pedaling up and down.

"Glad you like it, son," said his father. "Enjoy yourself. That's what life is for."

Just then Mrs. Jones came out and asked him to mow the lawn.

"You might help me in the garden a little, too," she said. "I can't do all that heavy work alone."

Mr. Jones got up to get the lawn mower. Then he saw that George was turning the wheels of his wagon, and once in a while pouring some sand over it.

"No, no, that's not the way to play with a wagon," said Mr. Jones. "You've got it upside down. Here." And he turned it right side up.

George thought that was a good idea, and he started filling the wagon with sand.

"No, no," said his father. "You don't understand. A wagon is to pull. Come on, I'll give you a ride."

Forgetting all about mowing the lawn, Mr. Jones put George in the wagon and pulled him out onto the sidewalk, and walked up and down a few times. George liked that fine. But pretty soon Mr. Jones got tired of pulling George around, and he went back to read the magazines.

George didn't like that at all. "Daddy pull wagon," he said, sitting there ready to cry.

"No more, now," said his father.

"Pull wagon," said George, loudly.

"Later," said his father, and took him back to the sand pile.

"Wow!" roared George.

"What's the matter?" Mrs. Jones asked, putting her head out of the kitchen where she was preparing supper.

"He wants me to keep on pulling him up and down," said Mr. Jones. "Here I've been working hard all week, and now I think I deserve a little rest."

"Well, maybe you do, but *I* can't amuse him now. I have to get supper. Where's William? William!"

William came to see what she wanted.

"Couldn't you amuse the baby for a little while?" his mother asked. "You've been playing with that beautiful bike all afternoon, and now I think you could mind your little brother just until suppertime."

So William dragged the wagon and George back out to the sidewalk where Patsy was having a turn riding the bike.

"I have to mind him," said William, looking glum. "I don't see why Daddy couldn't leave him in the sand pile. He would have gone on spinning the wheels. Now he knows about riding in the wagon and he'll want to do that all the time."

He pulled George up and down while Patsy rode the bike. After a while he got tired.

"I think it's my turn to ride the bike now," he said. "You pull George for a while."

Patsy looked at George. He was a fat baby.

She didn't feel much like pulling him. It was more fun to ride.

"I'll think of something," she said.

And just then she did. She jumped off and ran to the trash can where Mrs. Jones had dumped a lot of things from the tool shed. She pulled out a piece of rope and ran back. Then she tied the rope to the axle of the bike, and to the handle of the wagon.

"Now we have a trailer," she cried. "We can both ride and pull George."

William got on the bike and Patsy stood on the back, and off they went, pulling George slowly in the trailer.

George was happy. He sat holding on with his fat little fists.

"Pull wagon," he said.

CHAPTER 6

Mrs. McGinis Moves In

At last the time came that Patsy and William had been waiting for. George was in bed, supper was over, the lights were on in the houses. It wasn't quite dark outside. There was just a blueness over everything. Fireflies winked on and off. Aunt Geneva was in the living room crocheting a tablecloth.

"May I go out now?" Patsy asked.

"Oh, no, Patricia," said Aunt Geneva. "It's too late."

"Please," said Patsy, "just for a little while. I promised William."

"Well, all right," said Aunt Geneva. "But don't go far."

Over in William's house, he was asking the same thing.

"Can I go out? Please! I promised Patsy."

"Well, all right, but come right back."

Patsy was standing on the back step when William came along. She had a basket with a soft silk scarf in the bottom. This was to carry the kittens in. She had borrowed the scarf from Aunt Geneva. It was the softest thing she could find, and Patsy thought that if Aunt Geneva could know how sweet the kittens were, she wouldn't mind having her scarf used for their bed. William had a flashlight and a piece of fish for Mrs. McGinis.

They tiptoed through the grass to the side

porch, William lighting the way with the flashlight. Mrs. McGinis was there waiting for them. She walked up and down waving her tail in the air.

"Meow!" she said.

William held out the fish and she grabbed it. She was pretty hungry. Then Patsy reached in and lifted out the kittens and put them in the basket. They were soft and warm and very little and they clung to her hands with their tiny claws. They squeaked. When Mrs. McGinis heard them, she gulped down the fish and ran back and forth meowing anxiously.

"Everything is going to be all right," Patsy told her. "Just don't worry."

They carried the basket of kittens across the garden to the tool shed. William opened the door and they put the kittens on the sofa on an old blanket that George didn't need any more. Mrs.

McGinis jumped up on the sofa and gave each of the kittens a lick to make sure they were all right. Then she jumped down and ran around investigating the place. William opened the window so she could get out, and Patsy shone the light all around.

As William bent down to pat Mrs. McGinis,

she licked his fingers where they smelled of fish.

"I bet she's still hungry," said Patsy. "She didn't have much supper. You'd better get her something more to eat."

So William went to the house. In a few minutes Patsy heard him coming back. His mother was with him.

95

"Now, really, William," she was saying, "I insist on knowing what this is all about. Taking chicken out of the refrigerator at this time of night! And you'll get your feet all wet in this damp grass. I really must get your father to mow the lawn. Goodness! I can't do a thing with him!"

The door opened and they came in. William had a chicken leg in his hand. Mrs. McGinis ran to him and sniffed it.

"William!" said Mrs. Jones. "So it was for the cat! Really, children, this must stop! The idea of giving roast chicken to the cat!"

Then she saw the kittens on the sofa.

"And she's got *kittens!* Well, this is *too* much! We just can't have kittens. They will have to go tomorrow."

"But they just came," said Patsy.

"Where did they come from?" Mrs. Jones

asked. "How did they ever get in here?"

"We brought them," said Patsy. "They were under my side porch, and of course they couldn't stay there. So we cleaned out the tool shed——"

"So that's why you wanted the tool shed," said Mrs. Jones. "And what about George? If he gets hold of them, the mother cat will surely scratch him."

"Well, he can't open the door," said William, "and if we don't tell him it will be all right. Please let us keep them, Mother, *please!*"

"Oh, dear, you children, what won't you think of next?" said Mrs. Jones.

"It wasn't our idea," said Patsy. "It was Mrs. McGinis who thought of having the kittens. But we promised her we'd help her take care of them."

"Well, then you will have to do it," said Mrs.

Jones. "But you must keep this shed clean. And you must see that they get enough to eat, and when they get old enough you'll have to find homes for them. I can't do it. I have too much to do as it is."

"Oh, thank you," said Patsy and William. "We promise."

"Well, come along now," said Mrs. Jones. "I suppose now that that cat has sniffed that piece of chicken, she might as well have it. And you'd better give her something to drink. Get a dish of water and one of milk. Hurry, now."

Patsy and William ran to the house and brought some milk and water and set the dishes on the floor. Mrs. McGinis ran to the milk and lapped it up eagerly. Then she took a sip of water. Then she jumped up on the sofa to lie down beside her babies. She licked them all. As they crawled over to her side and nuzzled around to get their supper, she lifted her head and purred.

"Thank you," she seemed to be saying. "Thank you for this lovely house. It's just what I've always wanted."

CHAPTER 7

It Isn't Easy to Find Homes for Kittens

Mrs. McGinis was very happy in her new home. She had no trouble going in or out. She leaped gracefully onto a table and out through the window onto an orange crate that stood underneath.

She didn't go near the house. She seemed to remember George. And George remembered her. One day he caught sight of her leaping after a grasshopper in a corner of the garden.

"Oh! Pussy!" he cried joyfully. And then he rubbed his arm and said, "Pussy scwatch!"

He didn't try to catch her. He preferred his turtle. He spent hours watching the turtle crawl about in its tub. He liked to pat it on its shell and see it pull itself in and shut itself up tight. And sometimes he would take it for a walk. He would put it in the grass and let it walk awhile and then he would put it back in the tub.

"Turkle go home," he would say.

The kittens were growing fast. First they opened their eyes. Then they learned to stagger about on the sofa. They were very pretty kittens. One had a white bib and mittens. His name was Bibby. Another had one white ear and a white spot on the tip of his tail, so they called him Tippy. And the third was all gray like his mother. His name was Mickey.

One day as they were wrestling together on the sofa, one of them jumped too hard on his brothers and they all fell off. Of course they weren't hurt. Because they were so fat and furry they just bounced. But after that Patsy and William made them a bed in an old fruit basket on the floor. The basket had been a present to Aunt Geneva once long ago when she went on a trip. It still had a pink satin ribbon tied on the handle. Patsy thought that if Aunt Geneva could see how pretty it looked with the three kittens in it she would change her mind about cats. After all, if George wasn't too young to learn that cats scratch, maybe Aunt Geneva wasn't too old to learn that kittens are nice. Well, one of these days something might happen.

Now that the kittens had a bed on the floor, they were all over the little house. The children had to be careful in opening the door in order not to let them get out.

The kittens were eating a lot, too. When Patsy or William brought Mrs. McGinis' food her babies would line up and push their heads into the dish. They also learned to drink her milk. So after that William and Patsy brought two saucers of milk, one for Mrs. McGinis and one for the kittens.

One day William's mother looked into the re-frigerator and said, "What has happened to all the milk? There isn't enough for supper."

"Well, the kittens got awfully thirsty," William explained.

"What! Have you been feeding those kittens? Well, if they're big enough to eat from a dish, they'll have to be given away. I can't afford to feed four cats."

"Oh, Mother, we can't give them away yet," William exclaimed. "They're just getting to be fun to play with."

"That's too bad," said his mother. "But you'll have to find homes for them."

"If Patsy and I pay for their food out of our allowance," said William, "may we keep them a little longer?"

"Well, all right," said his mother, "but not too long. Ever since that Mrs. McGinis arrived it's been one thing after another. I wonder what will happen next."

William told Patsy what his mother had said. Patsy went to her room and got her purse. There was a quarter in it. William had seven cents. They went to the store.

"Please give us a bottle of milk and a can of cat food," Patsy said.

The man put the things in a bag and said, "Thirty-eight cents, please."

Patsy counted all the money they had. It wasn't enough.

"What shall we do?" William asked.

"You could buy canned milk instead of fresh,"

said the man. "That will be fifteen cents a can and fifteen for the cat food makes thirty, instead of thirty-eight."

So they did that. But as they were walking home with the cans, Patsy said, "My goodness, what are we going to do tomorrow? And the next day? We'll have to have thirty cents every single day! I didn't know it cost such a lot of money to feed cats!"

William nodded. "I guess my mother knew what she was talking about," he said sadly. "We'll have to give away the kittens."

"I guess so," said Patsy. She felt sad too. She had all she could do not to cry. "I'll think of something," she said to herself. But for once it didn't seem as if she could.

They asked William's mother to open the cans for them, and they fed the cats. The kittens were very hungry. They were in such a hurry to get

to their dinner that they knocked each other over and rolled on the floor. After they had eaten, they felt very good. They jumped on their mother and bit her ears and tail and she played with them until she got tired. Then she batted them gently with her paw and they went under the sofa and pretended to be fierce lions out hunting. They lashed their little pointed tails and pounced on the shadows on the floor.

Patsy and William watched them for a while. Soon Patsy said, "Well, come on. If we have to find homes for them we might as well do it now."

"How shall we do it?" William asked.

"Why, we'll just go to people's houses and ask if they want a kitten. There are lots of people on this block who don't have cats. Then we'll pick out the best homes and let those people have one."

"Why don't you take one?" William asked.

"I wish I could," said Patsy. "But Aunt Geneva still doesn't like cats. Of course the time may come when she'll change her mind, but it hasn't come yet."

They went down the street and picked out a house that looked like a good home for a kitten. Patsy rang the bell.

When a lady came to the door, Patsy said, "We're looking for a home for three nice kittens. Do you want one? They're gray, and one has white——"

"No," said the lady, slamming the door.

Patsy and William were very much surprised. "She wasn't polite," said Patsy. "She interrupted me in the middle of a sentence."

They went on to the next house. The lady there was nicer, but she didn't want a kitten either.

"We have two dogs," she said. "A kitten would not be happy here."

They went on to the third house. "Goodness, don't bring any cats around here," said the lady there.

At the next place, as soon as Patsy mentioned kittens, the lady said, "Oh, do you want a kitten? Take all you want," and pointed to a basket in which there were four.

They went around the corner. "Gracious me, what next," said that lady, whose hands were covered with dough. "I'm right in the middle of a pie. Go away, like good children."

"What does she mean, she's right in the middle of a pie?" William asked.

"She was making a pie," said Patsy. "That's the way grownups talk."

They went on to a house with a big yard. There were three children playing house under a tree. Patsy called out to them, "Hi! Do any of you want some kittens?"

This time they got the first sensible answer they had had all afternoon.

"Sure," said the children, coming to the fence. "What color are they?"

"They're gray," said William. "One has a white bib and mittens, and one has a white ear and tail."

"They must be darling," said the biggest girl. "Okay, we'll come with you." But just then their mother put her head out of an upstairs window and called, "Where are you going?"

"We're going to get some kittens," said the girl.

"No, indeed you're not," said the mother. "We have enough animals right now." So the children had to go back and play house some more.

"You want to play?" they asked.

But Patsy and William shook their heads.

"No, thanks," said Patsy. "Maybe some other time."

"Well, if our mother changes her mind we'll let you know," said the children.

"Okay," said Patsy and William.

They walked slowly home. They were tired. It certainly was not easy to find good homes for kittens.

CHAPTER 8

Aunt Geneva
Changes Her Mind

Now what were they going to do? How could they get enough money to pay fifteen cents a day for a can of milk and fifteen cents for a can of cat food?

"I've got an idea," said Patsy. "Let's get jobs."

"Okay," said William. "How do we do that?"

"Well, we go to ladies' houses and ask them if they have any jobs for us," said Patsy.

"Okay," said William. "Only let's not start

with that lady who slammed the door. I don't like her."

"Okay, let's go the other way," said Patsy. So they started off in the other direction. They rang the bell, and pretty soon a lady came out.

"We're looking for a job," Patsy explained to her. "Do you have any jobs for us?"

"Why, you sweet little things!" said the lady. "Let me see. You can sweep the front steps." And she gave them a broom. Patsy and William took turns sweeping, and when they were through the lady gave them each a slice of chocolate layer cake.

"This is for your pay," she said.

Patsy and William had each taken a bite— it was very good cake—so they couldn't give it back and explain that they wanted to be paid in money. They thanked the lady and said goodby.

"We'd better explain next time," said Patsy, "or we'll be eating cake all afternoon."

So at the next house they said to the lady, "We need to have some money to buy food so could you give us a job?"

The lady opened her eyes very wide and looked surprised.

"Gracious!" she said. "The idea of such young children having to earn money for food! Don't your parents give you enough to eat?"

"Oh, of course," said Patsy. "This is for the cats. We have to feed four cats."

"Well, I need to have the lawn mowed," said the lady. "But you're too small for that. All right, you can go to the store for me. I need two quarts of milk, a box of sugar, a can of peaches and a loaf of bread. Here is the money."

Patsy and William started for the store. It was a long walk, and they had to stand at the counter while the man waited on some big children and several ladies. Finally it was their turn. The man gave them two packages. William had the milk and the bread, and Patsy had the sugar and the peaches. The packages were heavy.

"This is pretty hard work," said William. "Do you suppose we'll have to do it every day?"

"Only until we find homes for the kittens," said Patsy.

"Well, I hope we find them soon," said William.

When they had delivered the groceries, the lady gave them each five cents.

"My goodness," said William as they walked away, "how many times do we have to do that before we get enough?"

"Three times," said Patsy, who could do arithmetic.

"Well, I'm tired," said William. He sat down on the curb.

Suddenly Patsy had an idea. "I know what we can do," she said. "We can take your new bike and ride it to the store."

"And how would we carry the groceries?" William asked.

"Why, we'd pull them in the trailer," said

Patsy. "It's nap time, so George doesn't need it."

So they got the tricycle and the trailer and went looking for more orders.

But no more ladies wanted groceries. Most of the ladies did their marketing early in the morning.

William and Patsy looked at each other and sighed. Earning money was a very hard thing.

"Now I see why my father is so tired every day," said William.

"Yes," said Patsy, "I guess it's better to be a lady and stay home than to be a man and have to go and earn money all the time. I guess I'll be a lady when I grow up."

"You're lucky," said William. "But how are we going to earn money now?"

"We'll have to think of something," said Patsy.

So they both sat down on the curb and thought. Patsy tried hard to think of the different ways in which people earned money. Some people went to an office every day. Some people worked in stores. There was a man who came around selling brushes. Maybe if she and William could find some brushes they could sell them, but she had no idea where they could find brushes.

"I'm sure I'll think of something," she said. And suddenly she did. "William!" she said. "If we had a hurdy-gurdy, we could play it and people would give us money."

"Sure," said William, "but where can we get one?"

"I know," said Patsy. "We'll get that old phonograph we found in the tool shed. We'll put it on the trailer and go around and play it, and people will give us money!"

"That's a fine idea," said William.

They hurried home and got the little phonograph, and loaded it on the wagon. Patsy ran to her house and found some of her records. William wound up the phonograph and Patsy started it playing. A tinkly piano played *Jingle Bells, Jingle Bells, Jingle All the Way*. It did indeed sound like a real hurdy-gurdy.

William got on the tricycle and pedaled slowly along the sidewalk, while Patsy walked alongside to make sure that the phonograph didn't fall off. Suddenly something furry came racing after them. It was Mrs. McGinis.

"Mrrow!" she said, and jumped up into the wagon. She sat down beside the phonograph and looked around, very pleased.

"What a funny thing to do," said Patsy. "She must like music! Go on, William, let's give her a ride."

So William pedaled slowly around the corner. When the record was finished, Mrs. McGinis looked up at Patsy and said, "Meow!"

"She wants us to play more," said Patsy, and she put on another record. This one was *Home on the Range,* and it was quite loud. Some children came out to see what was playing.

"Oh, look, it's a hurdy-gurdy!" they shouted, and they followed it along the street. "Look at the cat sitting in the wagon!"

They laughed and sang. The children and the hurdy-gurdy together made so much noise that some ladies came out and told them to go away.

"You'll wake up the babies!" they said.

William pedaled on. More and more children

121

began following them, and more ladies came out to tell them to go away and not make so much noise. But nobody thought of giving them any money.

Suddenly they heard somebody calling, "William! Patsy! Where are you?" It was William's

mother. She came running after them. "Goodness, children, what in the world are you doing?"
she asked. "All the mothers in the block are tele-
phoning me. The idea of making all that noise
at naptime! Stop it at once!"

Patsy switched off the phonograph. "We were

doing it to earn money to feed the cats," she explained. "But we didn't get any money."

"I should think not," said Mrs. Jones. "What next? Come home at once. And stop playing that phonograph, please."

Patsy and William started wearily homeward. Suddenly Mrs. Jones gave a start.

"My gracious!" she exclaimed. "I forgot all about George! I left him all alone in the garden! Goodness knows what he'll do!" And she began to run.

William pedaled as fast as he could to keep up, and Patsy ran alongside. Mrs. McGinis jumped out of the wagon and ran too. When they got to the garden, George was nowhere in sight.

"Oh, my goodness, where is he?" Mrs. Jones cried, very much excited. "He's probably fallen down the cellar, or he's run out in the street and gotten lost!"

They ran around the garden, looking behind all the bushes. No George.

But suddenly Patsy noticed something. The door of the tool shed was open.

"Maybe he's in there," she said.

"Oh, dear, those cats will scratch him!" exclaimed Mrs. Jones, and she ran as fast as she could to the tool shed. Mrs. McGinis ran too, as if she were afraid something might happen to her children.

Patsy and William hurried after. They peeped in and saw a most unusual sight.

There sat George on the floor, with his fat legs stuck straight out in front of him. In his lap was Tippy, the kitten with the white ear and tail.

"Nice liddle pussy," he was saying, patting the kitten's fur.

The turtle was crawling around on the floor. William pushed the door open a little farther,

and there on the sofa they saw—of all people—
Aunt Geneva. She was knitting. And in her lap
she was holding Bibby, the kitten with the white
bib and mittens. He had his eyes closed and he

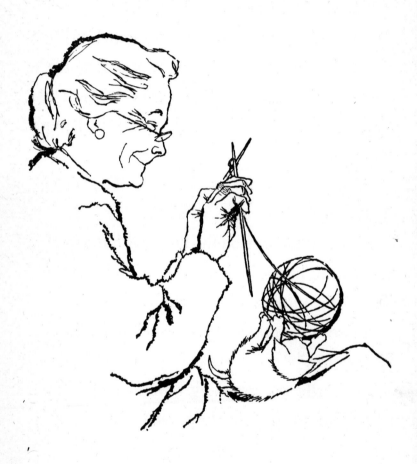

was purring. On the floor was Mickey, the all-gray kitten, playing with Aunt Geneva's shoe-laces!

Patsy and William and Mrs. Jones were so surprised that they couldn't say a word. Mrs. McGinis was the first to speak.

"Meow!" she said, and she ran and gave each of her children a lick to make sure they were all right. Then she went and sat down beside George.

George looked at her. But he didn't pull her tail. It seemed as if he had learned how to behave with cats.

"Why, Miss Geneva!" said Mrs. Jones. "Imagine finding you here!"

"George came into our garden through the hole in the fence," said Aunt Geneva. "He was taking the turtle for a walk and it ran away. So I brought him back and we found the door open and three kittens asleep in my old fruit basket. I was wondering where that was."

And she cast on more stitches. The kitten in her lap woke up and reached a white paw for the thread. His claws got stuck in it and made quite a snarl but Aunt Geneva didn't get angry. She just smiled and untangled him.

"Why, Aunt Geneva," said Patsy, "I thought you said you didn't like cats."

Aunt Geneva laughed. "Well, I really don't," she said, "but you see this isn't a cat, it's a kitten."

"Do you like kittens?"

Aunt Geneva smiled foolishly. "They *are* cute," she admitted.

Patsy thought to herself, "People are funny. Doesn't she know kittens grow up to be cats?" But she didn't say so. Instead she asked, "Well, can't we have one, then?"

Aunt Geneva looked very undecided for a

while, as if she were having an argument with herself. At last she said, "Well, I see you won't be happy until you do. Which one shall we take?"

Patsy picked up Mickey from the floor and held him beside Bibby to see which one was nicer.

"I like them both," she said.

Aunt Geneva sighed. "So do I," she said. "I can't decide which to take. And one kitten would be lonesome. Let's take two."

CHAPTER 9

The Hurdy-Gurdy Man Comes Back

Patsy and Aunt Geneva took the kittens home. They took the fruit basket too, because after all it was Aunt Geneva's, and they put it in the kitchen for the kittens to sleep in. But Mickey and Bibby didn't stay there. In no time they were exploring the house. They scampered into the living room. They went tearing around under the table, pulling at the fringe of the tablecloth, climbing on the sofa and playing tag over the tops of the chairs. They had had a sofa and chairs all their own in the tool shed, so of course they thought that sofas and chairs were made for kittens to play tag on.

Then they pulled down all the mats as they pushed each other around. Aunt Geneva didn't get angry. She watched Bibby stick a white paw out from under the sofa and bat at Mickey, who was reaching for him from the seat, and she just laughed till tears came to her eyes.

"Aunt Geneva," Patsy said, "aren't you afraid they'll spoil your mats?"

Aunt Geneva wiped her eyes and said, "Patricia, I guess a couple of lively kittens are more important than a lot of old pieces of cotton." And she gathered up all the mats and stuffed them into a drawer.

Patsy was more and more surprised at her aunt. "I didn't know you liked kittens so much," she said.

"I guess I never knew it either," said Aunt Geneva, "till I saw them in that basket with the pink bow. It just goes to show you're never too old to learn."

Patsy agreed with her, but she thought it showed something else too. It showed that nobody could resist three darling kittens in a basket with a pink bow. Suddenly she had an idea.

"I know how to find a home for the third kitten," she said. "May we borrow the basket?"

"All right," said Aunt Geneva, "but bring it back."

Patsy carried the basket to William's yard. "We'll put Tippy in it," she said, "and carry him around. Somebody will be sure to want him."

They had to get the kitten away from George. George didn't want to give him up, but they showed him how to put his turtle in the wagon

and pull it around, and he was happy to do
that.

"That turtle certainly has come in handy,"
said Patsy, as they started down the street with
Tippy in the basket.

"Let's not go to that lady who slammed the

door," said William, as they came in sight of her house.

But just as they were hurrying past, the lady came out.

"What have you got there, children?" she asked. Then she looked into the basket. "Oh, what a darling kitten! Where are you going with it?"

"We're going to find a home for it," said William.

"Well, it's so cute, maybe I could take it," said the lady.

"But you said before you didn't want one," said Patsy.

"Oh, but that was before I saw it," said the lady. "Have you any others?"

"No, this is the last one," said William.

"Then I *must* have it," said the lady.

But just then along came the lady who had

been making pie the day William and Patsy went to her house.

"Oh, what a sweet kitten!" she said. "Are you giving it away? I'd love a kitten like this. May I have it?"

William was confused. He looked from one lady to the other and didn't know what to say. It was pretty hard to say no to two grown-up ladies.

But Patsy thought fast. "We'll let you know," she said.

"Oh, all right," said the ladies. Patsy and William went on around the corner to the house where the three children lived.

"Look," said Patsy, "we only have one left. Do you want it?"

"Oh, boy," said the biggest girl. "Our mother hasn't changed her mind yet, but give us the basket and we'll see what we can do." She took the basket with Tippy in it and they ran into the house. Pretty soon they were back. The basket was empty.

"Our mother changed her mind," said the biggest girl. "As soon as she saw the kitten and we told her it was the last one, she said all right."

William and Patsy walked home, swinging the empty basket.

"Isn't it funny," said Patsy, "that when we had three to give away, nobody wanted them. But when it was the last one, they all wanted it."

"People are funny," said William. But he looked sad. Patsy knew what was the matter with him. He didn't like to think that there would be no more family in the tool shed.

"You can come over and see Bibby and Mickey," she said.

But William shook his head. It wasn't the same thing at all.

"You still have Mrs. McGinis," she reminded him. "And maybe she'll have more kittens." That cheered him up a little.

When they sat down to rest on the curb in front of William's house, Mrs. McGinis came out to greet them. She rubbed her head against William's arm and climbed into his lap.

"Meow!" she said.

"She misses the kittens too," he said.

"You can both come and visit them," said Patsy. "After all, she's their mother, and maybe Aunt Geneva will even learn to like cats too."

"Okay," said William. And Mrs. McGinis nestled down in his arms and purred.

As they sat there resting, they suddenly heard a faint sound of music. It tinkled gaily at the end of the street.

"It's the hurdy-gurdy!" said Patsy. "At last it's

coming back to our street. I'll go and get some money for the man."

As she was about to go indoors, Mrs. McGinis suddenly did a strange thing. She jumped out of William's lap and ran up the street toward the hurdy-gurdy. William and Patsy ran after her. They had never seen such a music-loving cat. They ran as fast as they could, and they were just in time to see Mrs. McGinis jump up on the hurdy-gurdy. The man held out his arms and she leaped into them.

"Petronella!" the man exclaimed. "You come back to me!" And he patted her and hugged her and, yes, he actually kissed her!

William walked up to him. "That's *my* cat!" he exclaimed.

The man looked surprised. "She—*my* cat," he said, stumbling as if he didn't speak English very well.

"No, no," said William angrily. "She lives in our house. She came to us. We fixed up a house for her. She had three kittens. You can't take her away!" He was almost crying.

The man looked more and more surprised. "I —lose cat," he stammered. "I come back—look-a for her. No find. Not know where she's go. Now I play music, she's run to me. She my cat."

Patsy looked at the man and at the gray cat in his arms.

"I guess he's right, William," she said. "Mrs. McGinis heard the music. That must be why she ran after us when we played the phonograph."

"But he's been back a couple of times," said William. "Why didn't she run after him then?"

Patsy shook her head. "He was always too far away," she said. "She couldn't hear him. I wonder why he never came to this street."

She turned to the man. "Why didn't you come back here?" she asked.

The man looked around anxiously at the houses and said, "Lady get mad. Say go away. So

I no come-a back. And my Petronella here all-a time." And he gave the cat another hug. She settled down and licked his thumb. She certainly looked contented.

William shut his lips hard so he wouldn't cry.

"Come on," said Patsy. "We'll show you her house." And she pulled the man by the sleeve.

"Alla right. I come." He put the cat on top of the hurdy-gurdy and picked up the handles. And William and Patsy led him along the street, then up the path and around to the back garden. There was the tool shed with the morning-glories and the tall grass all around.

"Here," said William, "here's her house."

As if to show that it really was her house, Mrs. McGinis leaped down from the hurdy-gurdy. She jumped up on the sofa and sat there looking at them and purring.

"She's got kittens," said Patsy. "Wait here, I'll show you." She ran through the hole in the fence into Aunt Geneva's kitchen. Snatching up Mickey and Bibby, she ran back. The man took the kittens in his hands and looked at them.

"Oh, she's-a have baby!" he said. "That's-a nice. You keep baby, I take Petronella."

"But I want Petronella—I mean Mrs. McGinis!" William shouted. He shouted so loudly that his mother came running from the kitchen to see what all the fuss was about.

"What in the world is going on here?" she asked. "Who is this?"

"It's the hurdy-gurdy man," Patsy started to explain. "He says Mrs. McGinis belongs to him——"

"And she doesn't!" William shouted, bursting into tears at last. "She's mine! The kittens are all gone and I won't give Mrs. McGinis to any-

body!" And he grabbed the cat and cried into her fur. Mrs. McGinis twisted herself around and looked at him.

"Meow!" she said.

"She likes you, William," said Patsy. "Don't cry."

"Yes, but she likes the hurdy-gurdy man too," William wailed.

"I wish I could understand what is going on here," said Mrs. Jones. "This cat just appeared from nowhere and we took her in. Now you say she belongs to this man."

The hurdy-gurdy man sighed. He put out his hand and stroked the cat. Then he said, "Lady, I tell-a you what happen. My Petronella, she live with me. But I no have house. I live in room. I no can leave my Petronella. So I take her with me when I go for play music. She ride on top. But Petronella, she have babies. She need house for babies. So she leave me. She come here. I go every day and look for her. I play music. I think, she hear music, she come back. And today I find her."

And, as if he were exhausted by this long speech, he took out his handkerchief and wiped his forehead.

William sniffed. He patted Mrs. McGinis. Then he said, "Well, okay. I guess she's your cat. You can have her." And he held out the cat to the man.

But the man shook his head sadly. "No," he said, "I no take Petronella. You fix nice little house for her. She stay here."

Patsy felt sorry for him. She didn't want him to take the cat away, but she couldn't help feeling sorry for the poor man who didn't have a house, only a room. Probably he lived all alone and had nobody to keep him company but the cat.

"I'll think of something," she said to herself. "I just *have* to."

The hurdy-gurdy man was talking to the cat. "Petronella," he said, "you stay here in this-a house. See, nice flowers!" And he reached out and plucked some dead leaves off the vine that hung over the doorway. Patsy remembered the flowers he had had in his coat the last time she saw him.

"You like flowers?" she said.

"Oh, sure," said the man, smiling at her. "In old country I—I dig, how you say——" And he made motions as if he were hoeing a garden.

"You're a gardener?" Patsy asked.

The man nodded. "This-a nice garden," he said, bowing to Mrs. Jones.

"It would be if I had a chance to work in it," she said.

Suddenly Patsy had an idea. "Mrs. Jones!" she

burst out. "Let the man stay here in the tool shed
with Petronella, I mean Mrs. McGinis, and he
can help you with the garden! Then William will

still have Mrs. McGinis, I mean Petronella. Whatever her name is."

William stared at her for a moment. Then he yelled, "Yippee! That's a real good idea!"

But the man and Mrs. Jones still had no idea of what she was talking about.

"Well, don't you see," William explained, "Daddy doesn't like to work in the garden. So this man could do it. He could mow the lawn, too. Daddy doesn't like that either. Mister, do you know how to mow a lawn?"

The man didn't understand a word.

"Cut the grass," said William. "Like this." And he made believe he was pushing a lawn mower across the grass.

The man nodded.

"See, Mother?" said William. "He knows how."

"But, William," said his mother, "we can't just

invite a strange man to come and live in our tool shed."

"Why not?" said William. "After he lives here he won't be strange."

"Well, we'll speak to your father and see what he thinks of it," said Mrs. Jones. She always said that when she couldn't decide about something.

"Goody," said William, "here he comes now."

And sure enough, there was Mr. Jones coming up the walk. He had an armful of books that he had bought somewhere.

"Daddy!" cried William, running to him. "Here's a man who knows how to run a lawn mower. Can he stay in our tool shed with Mrs. McGinis and be our gardener?"

"What!" said his father. "You mean I don't have to cut the grass any more?"

"Any more!" said his mother. "You never *do* do it."

"Well, then I guess we do need a gardener, if I'm as bad as all that," said Mr. Jones. "Can the man do anything else besides push a lawn mower?"

"Yes," said Patsy, "he can play a hurdy-gurdy."

"Just what we need, I'm sure," said Mr. Jones. "I mean does he know anything else about gardening?"

"He likes flowers," said Patsy.

The hurdy-gurdy man was looking from one to the other, trying to figure out what it was all about. They were talking too fast for him. He wiped his forehead again with the handkerchief.

"What is your name?" Mr. Jones asked him.

"Me—Tony," said the man. "Tony Lazzarro."

"All right, Mr. Lazzarro," said Mr. Jones. "Come over here. We have to have a little talk. Just man to man, you know. We men have to stick together." And he took the man over to another corner of the garden and they talked in low voices.

After a while they came back. Both of them were grinning.

"Patsy had a very good idea," said Mr. Jones. "Maybe something can be worked out. I think we do need a gardener."

"But, dear——" said his wife.

"Now you know you have too much to do in the garden," said Mr. Jones, "and I've got all this reading to do."

"I don't see why you have to buy all that stuff," said Mrs. Jones.

"Why these are rare old books," said Mr. Jones, "and don't you put them in the tool shed, because that's where our gardener is going to live."

"Well, we'll see about it," said Mrs. Jones.

But Patsy and William noticed that she didn't say no.

CHAPTER 10

The Hurdy-Gurdy Man Comes to Stay

They did see about it. And after a while it was arranged for Mr. Lazzarro to move into the tool shed.

First, of course, Patsy and William had to fix it up for him. They swept it clean, they put fresh flowers into the jam jars, and Aunt Geneva gave them some curtains for the windows and the glass door.

Then they painted the table and the two wooden chairs bright red. Mrs. Jones got a small stove which just fitted in a corner and could be used for cooking, and for heating when the weather got cold. And she gave them some dishes which they arranged neatly on a shelf over the stove. It was a lovely house.

Then Mr. Lazzarro came. He brought his hurdy-gurdy, and his clothes tied up in a red checked tablecloth. (He had no suitcase.) And he brought several potted plants.

Mr. Lazzarro was very happy. In the mornings he worked in the garden or mowed the lawn. It wasn't long before the Joneses' garden was the most beautiful on all Elm Street. The flowers bloomed brightly and there wasn't a weed to be seen. And the grass was always neatly cut.

Mrs. Jones was very pleased. Now she could enjoy her garden. Mr. Jones was pleased too because he had plenty of time for his reading.

In the afternoons, when the weather was good,

Mr. Lazzarro took the hurdy-gurdy out with Mrs. McGinis perched on top. Up and down the streets they went, playing the merry tunes. But they went quietly past the houses where the babies were taking naps.

In the evenings, Mr. Lazzarro parked the hurdy-gurdy in front of his little house. After supper Patsy and William and their friends took turns playing it. Once in a while Mrs. Jones would let George stay up a little past his bedtime, and he would bring his turtle to hear the music. The kittens, Micky and Bibby, would run over to visit their mother. They didn't come through the hole in the fence, because Mr. Lazzarro had mended it and made a gate instead. But kittens don't care about gates. They just climbed over the fence.

They played with their mother's tail and had pretend-boxing matches with each other.

Mr. Lazzarro would sit in the doorway of his little house and smile at the children and the animals. Mrs. McGinis, sitting proudly at his feet, would purr as if she thought all this was something she had arranged.

"And maybe she did," said Patsy. "But I must say we helped. That was a pretty good idea we had, wasn't it, William?"